Temper Temper

Nicola Morgan

Fitzhenry & Whiteside

Temper Temper

Fitzhenry & Whiteside
195 Allstate Parkway
Markham, Ontario L3R 4T8

Designed by Ian Gillen
Typesetting by ISIS Communications

Canadian Cataloguing in Publication Data

Morgan, Nicola, 1959 —
   Temper, temper
ISBN 0-88902-559-2
I. Title

PS8576.0736T45 1988   jC813'.54   C88-093661-4
PZ7.M67Te 1988

For Sophie, who inspired me all the way.

When Mabel Babelman was about the tiniest a tiny baby could be, she would gurgle and goo and smile so sweetly.

Everyone who saw her agreed. She was the loveliest baby they had ever seen.

Sometimes Mr. and Mrs. Babelman were busy and they would put little Mabel down on her mat to play. Mabel would giggle and goo, but nobody paid any attention. Instead, Mabel found herself all alone.

Suddenly a strange thing
happened...

Temper Temper

Mabel grew bigger and learned all sorts of wonderful things.

She could walk and talk. When Mrs. Babelman went shopping she would let Mabel push the cart. People would stop and smile. They had never seen such a helpful little girl.

Sometimes Mabel would
go too fast — *watch out* —

Temper Temper

Mabel grew older. She was still not old enough to go to school, but she was allowed to spend the whole day at her Grandmother's house. Mabel and Granny Babelman would do special things together. Mabel liked telling stories and baking cookies best.

But, sometimes the cookies
burned — and so did Mabel.

Temper Temper

Mabel grew big enough to start school and she made lots of new friends. Everyone liked the teacher, Mr. Weatherhead, because he was always smiling…

… except when he gave
Mabel back her spelling test —

Temper Temper

It seemed as though a
strange thing kept happening
to Mabel. Whenever she became
angry, Mabel would vanish…

… and in her place would appear the most terrifying terrible *Temper Temper Monster*.

Mabel noticed that something was wrong. Nobody wanted to play with her anymore.

Mrs. Babelman said it was easier to do the shopping alone and even Granny Babelman didn't want to see Mabel. She was worried because her cat was still hiding in the basement.

Mabel was all alone.

"I'm going to catch the Temper Temper Monster and make it behave!" thought Mabel to herself. She snuck into the bathroom to wait.

Mabel waited and waited and waited and waited, and just when she thought she would scream, the terrible *Temper Temper Monster* suddenly appeared.

Mabel had never seen anything so scarey before, and she fell right off the bathroom stool.

"I'm all alone," thought Mabel, looking around. "Where did the Temper Temper Monster go?"

Suddenly it all made sense. Mabel began to laugh. She laughed and laughed. Mabel laughed so hard she could hardly stop.

At school the next day, while Mabel was trying to spell a very difficult word at the front of the class, the ***Temper Temper Monster*** appeared. The classroom became very quiet. Everyone looked nervously around.

Then suddenly…

… Mabel started to laugh, and the Temper Temper Monster disappeared. The other children stared, but Mabel was laughing so hard that everyone, even Mr. Weatherhead, joined in. Never had spelling been so much fun.

After school Mabel went to her Grandmother's and tried to coax the cat to come out of the basement.

"Kitty, Kitty, come up and play," called Mabel in her sweetest voice. The cat wouldn't budge and Mabel felt herself getting angry.

Suddenly Granny Babelman found herself face to face with the terrible ***Temper Temper Monster***.

But Mabel quickly laughed away the Temper Temper Monster. Granny Babelman started to chuckle, and finally the cat came out of the basement to see what was going on.

The next day Mr. and
Mrs. Babelman had some
shopping to do and they
decided that Mabel could
come along. She was being
very helpful, pushing the
shopping cart. All of a sudden
— SMASH!! — A very rude lady
came around the corner right into
the *Temper Temper Monster*.

Everyone looked worried,
but Mabel knew what to do.
She laughed and laughed. The
Temper Temper Monster quickly
disappeared. Before long almost
everyone in the store was laughing
as well.

Once again everyone who saw Mabel agreed. She was the loveliest little girl to be around. She could make people smile and laugh, and everyone wanted to be her friend. She hardly ever got angry anymore, and the terrible *Temper Temper Monster*...

…was **almost** never seen again!

Printed and bound in Hong Kong